TORTOISE AND HARE

A Fairy Tale to Help You Find Balance

words by
SUSAN VERDE

pictures by
JAY FLECK

Abrams Books for Young Readers
New York

To my beautiful yoga teachers Alex B. and Alison B.,
who always help me find balance on and off the mat
—S.V.

To Owen
—J.F.

The illustrations for this book were made in pencil and colored digitally.

Cataloging-in-Publication Data has been applied for and may be obtained from the Library of Congress.

ISBN 978-1-4197-4954-4

Text © 2022 Susan Verde
Illustrations © 2022 Jay Fleck
Book design by Heather Kelly

Printed and bound in China
10 9 8 7 6 5 4 3 2 1

Abrams Books for Young Readers are available at special
discounts when purchased in quantity for premiums and promotions
as well as fundraising or educational use. Special editions can also be created to specification.
For details, contact specialsales@abramsbooks.com or the address below.

Abrams® is a registered trademark of Harry N. Abrams, Inc.

ABRAMS The Art of Books
195 Broadway, New York, NY 10007
abramsbooks.com

Once upon a time there were two neighbors, Hare and Tortoise. Although they lived side by side, they each did things very differently.

Hare did *everything* quickly.
There was so much to do every day. Hare liked to get it all done—
and fast!

Each morning, she made her bed in a jiffy.
(Although sometimes it looked like there
was someone still sleeping there.)

She got dressed and ready for her busy day
in no time at all. (Although sometimes she
missed a button or two.)

She planted her garden in a flash.
(Although sometimes she couldn't remember
where she planted her tomatoes.)

She ate her meals with gusto.
(Although sometimes she got a tummy ache.)

She was even a speed reader!
(Although sometimes she couldn't
remember what her books were about!)

Hare was always so busy that she didn't
pay attention to the things around her.

She didn't even stop to say "hello" to those she passed by,
in too much of a hurry to notice a wave or hear the latest gossip.

Some might say she was *too* fast.

Now, Tortoise did *everything* slowly and carefully.
There was so much to do, and Tortoise liked to take his sweet time
with it all.

Each morning, he meticulously made his bed,
folding the sheets and tucking the corners.
(Although sometimes it looked like no one
had ever slept all snuggly in the bed.)

He got dressed with care, considering
colors, textures, and of course, the weather.
(Although sometimes he wasn't out of his
pajamas until way past morning.)

He planted his garden carefully,
making sure each seed was
in its proper place. (Although
sometimes he missed tomato
season altogether.)

He ate his meals in tiny bites, savoring each morsel. (Although sometimes it was dinnertime before he even finished lunch.)

He read his books leisurely, pondering every word. (Although sometimes he didn't get to the end of the story!)

Tortoise made sure to say hello to everyone he passed by, offering a cup of tea and asking them all kinds of questions.

Some might say he was *too* slow.

One day, Tortoise was sitting in his yard, looking up at the sky and watching the clouds make funny shapes.

Hare, in the meantime, had a to-do list! She was rushing around, getting things done, and furiously checking them off.

DONE!

DONE!

DONE!

TO-DO LIST
MOW LAWN ✓
WATER GARDEN ✓
TRIM BUSHES ✓

Out of the corner of her eye, Hare noticed Tortoise was barely moving. This irritated her quite a bit.

"Tortoise, don't you have anything to do? Why are you wasting the day just sitting there? Look at what I've already done!"

"Yes, Hare," Tortoise said slowly. "There are some things I need to do. But right now, I am enjoying my tea and looking at the lovely sky. Why don't you join me?"

Hare said, "There's no time for that!" and she kept on moving.

By nightfall, Tortoise was still sitting outside,
but now he was looking at the stars.

"Tortoise! You are so slow. How can you just sit there all day long? I bet you can't move fast for anything!"

"Well, Hare," Tortoise said slowly, "I think *you* are wrong. I am certain I could move faster if I wanted to. In fact, why don't we have a race? From here to town. I bet I can beat you, no problem."

Hare laughed as though she had never heard anything funnier. "You're *on*! The day after tomorrow! We will race from here to town. You'll see how fast I am and how slow you are."

Hare spent the whole next day running around her yard, doing jumping jacks, and getting ready to show off her incredible speed.

Tortoise spent the day sipping tea and putting on his special tracksuit.

Meanwhile, word had spread of the race, and the townspeople were buzzing with excitement!

Some said, "That Hare is too fast! She will surely beat slow Tortoise."

But some said, "If Tortoise challenged Hare, he *must* have a trick up his sleeve."

The day of the race arrived. Tortoise and Hare stood at the starting line.

"Ready.

Set.

GO!"

Hare was off in a flash. Tortoise began creeping slowly forward.

At the halfway mark, Hare knew she was way ahead. So she decided to take a quick nap, certain she would wake up before Tortoise even got close.

And indeed, Tortoise was way behind, moving very slowly. There was so much to see!

He stopped along the way to smell the flowers. He investigated every noise and paid close attention to the feeling of the road under his feet.

And he made sure to take the time to say hello to everyone he passed along the way (until they politely reminded him that he was in a race).

Meanwhile, Hare's quick nap had turned into a deep sleep. When a chill and her own loud snore finally woke her, it was dark out. *Well*, she thought, *I am sure I still have time to win this race. That Tortoise is so slow, he has probably stopped somewhere to count the pebbles in the road!*

She was about to take off again when she heard a voice next to her.

"Hello, Hare." It was Tortoise.
Hare was in shock! "Tortoise, what are you doing here?
How long have you been here?"

"Just a little while. I was going to keep moving to show you
how fast I can be, but you looked so peaceful, and the moon
is beautiful and shining so brightly that I just had to stop.
Look at all of those stars!"

Hare looked up. The beauty of the night sky, the cool air,
and Tortoise by her side made her stay very still.
It was something she hadn't done in a long, long time.

And in that moment, staring up at the sparkling,
magnificent stars, Hare realized that maybe it wasn't
so important to be fast all of the time. Maybe there were
times when it was good to slow down.

So together, Tortoise and Hare stayed right
in that spot, making wishes on the stars and
talking about their dreams, until at last . . .

. . . the sun was coming up.

"Tortoise," Hare said, "we need to finish this race. How would you like to go fast?"

"I would like that very much," said Tortoise.
With that, Hare put Tortoise on her back, and they sped toward the finish line.

And in *that* moment, as he felt the warmth of the wind on his face and the exhilarating beat of his heart, Tortoise realized that maybe it wasn't so important to be slow all of the time. Maybe there were times when it was good to be fast.

Tortoise and Hare joyfully
crossed the finish line together.

From then on, whenever Tortoise needed a little speed in picking out his outfits, planting his tomatoes, or even finishing a good book, Hare was there to help.

And when Hare needed to slow things down while making her bed, buttoning her buttons, or savoring a cup of tea while watching the clouds float by, Tortoise was there to help.

Because sometimes it's good to be fast,
and sometimes it's good to be slow—but mostly,
it's good to have a friend to help you find the balance.

AUTHOR'S NOTE

Have you ever done something so quickly that it didn't turn out the way you'd hoped? Or so slowly that you ran out of time? Have you ever put just the right amount of time and care into something—and it felt really good?

Just like Tortoise and Hare discovered, too much of anything doesn't always give the best results. Sometimes what we need is balance: just the right mix of fast and slow. And sometimes it takes a friend or two to help you find your "just right."

Here are a few of Tortoise and Hare's favorite activities to help you slow things down, feel energized, and find your balance—to be the best version of *you*!

TREE POSE: When you are feeling too fast, what better way is there to slow things down and find balance than a balancing pose? Stand up tall with two feet on the ground, chest proud, and shoulders relaxed. Find a spot to fix your gaze upon that is not moving, like a door handle or a spot on the wall (this is the trick to minimize the wobbles). Breathe in and out deeply through your nose. Bring your palms together by your heart. Now take one foot, place it against your ankle, and pause. Keep your focus on your spot, then slowly lift your foot higher on your standing leg, above your knee. Find stillness, and slowly reach your arms (branches) to the sky. Stay there for a moment, then repeat on the other side. This pose is also wonderful for pausing and pondering the beauty of nature as you imagine yourself as a majestic tree.

ENERGIZING BREATH: This breathing exercise can help when you are feeling too slow and you need to rev up your engine! Stand with your legs wide apart, toes turned out. Bend your knees a little, like you are riding a horse. Reach both arms out in front of you, make your hands into fists, and take a big breath in through your nose. As you breathe out, pull your elbows straight back by your sides, arms bent, fists turned up to the sky, and yell "HA!" Repeat this eight times. Next, raise your arms over your head, breathe in through your nose, and draw your elbows straight down to your sides, letting your breath out with a "HA!" Now repeat this sequence four times each, then two times each, and then finish with a few rounds of one "HA!" starting with arms out front and one "HA!" starting with arms overhead. Whenever you feel all "HA!"ed out, straighten your legs, let your arms relax, and notice your energy. Are you more energized? Is your heart beating faster? I bet you don't feel too slow anymore!

LIZARD ON A ROCK: This exercise not only has a funny name, but it is also fun because you get to do it with a friend. Start by deciding who is the rock and who is the lizard. Don't worry, you will eventually switch places! If you are the rock, get into child's pose: Kneel on the ground with your toes touching, knees a bit wider than your hips, and sit on your heels. Lean your body forward over your knees until your forehead touches the ground. Your arms can be by your sides or out in front of you. If you are the lizard, sit very gently at the foot of the rock facing in the opposite direction. Rest your back gently against the rock and lean your body all the way back, lying over the rock with your heart open to the sky. Let

your arms fall wide on either side of you. Once both the rock and lizard are settled, begin to breathe in and out slowly through your noses, and notice each other's breaths on your backs. See if you can make your breaths the same length and rhythm, finding the perfect mix of stretching and relaxation. When you are ready, change places. Just as Tortoise and Hare helped each other find balance, in this pose, you and your partner can help each other find balance, too.